THIS BOOK BELONGS TO:

TAILS FROM THE PANTRY

Little Life Lessons from Mom and Dad

SPUD

By Patsy Clairmont

Illustrated by Joni Oeltjenbruns

Tommy NELSON®

A Division of Thomas Nelson Publishers
Since 1798

www.thomasnelson.com

TAILS FROM THE PANTRY: SPUD
Text © 2006 by Patsy Clairmont
Illustrations © 2006 by Tommy Nelson®, a Division of Thomas Nelson, Inc.
All rights reserved. No portion of this book may be reproduced in any form
without the written permission of the publisher, with the exception of brief
excerpts in reviews.
Published in Nashville, Tennessee, by Tommy Nelson®, a Division of Thomas
Nelson, Inc.
Tommy Nelson books may be purchased in bulk for educational, business,
fundraising, or sales promotional use. For information, please e-mail
SpecialMarkets@ThomasNelson.com.

Library of Congress Cataloging-in-Publication Data

Clairmont, Patsy.
  Spud / by Patsy Clairmont ; illustrated by Joni Oeltjenbruns.
      p. cm. — (Tails from the pantry)
  Summary: Meatball, Soccer, and Stinky MacKenzie, mice who live in the
pantry, band together to fight off Spud, a rat with a reputation as a bully.
  ISBN 1-4003-0802-X (hardcover)
  [1. Bullies—Fiction. 2. Brothers and sisters—Fiction. 3. Mice—Fiction. 4. Rats—
Fiction.] I. Oeltjenbruns, Joni, ill. II. Title.
  PZ7.C5276Spu 2006
  [E]—dc22
                                          2005026840

Printed in the United States of America
06 07 08 09 10 WOR 9 8 7 6 5 4 3 2 1

This little series is dedicated to Justin and Noah. . . .

How blessed I am to have two "little mouse" grandsons who regularly nibble in my pantry. Darlings, leave all the crumbs you want in Nana's house. I'll tidy up later. Always heed Mommy and Daddy's lessons about staying safe. You are both loved "a bushel and a peck and a hug around the neck."

~Nana

*O*nce upon a sack of potatoes sat a rat named Spud. Spud was feared throughout the house as the garage bully. And when he heard that there was a family of mice living in the pantry, Spud came dressed for troublemaking. He pulled on his meanest look, he squeezed into his beady-eyed stare, and he wiggled his voice into a growl.

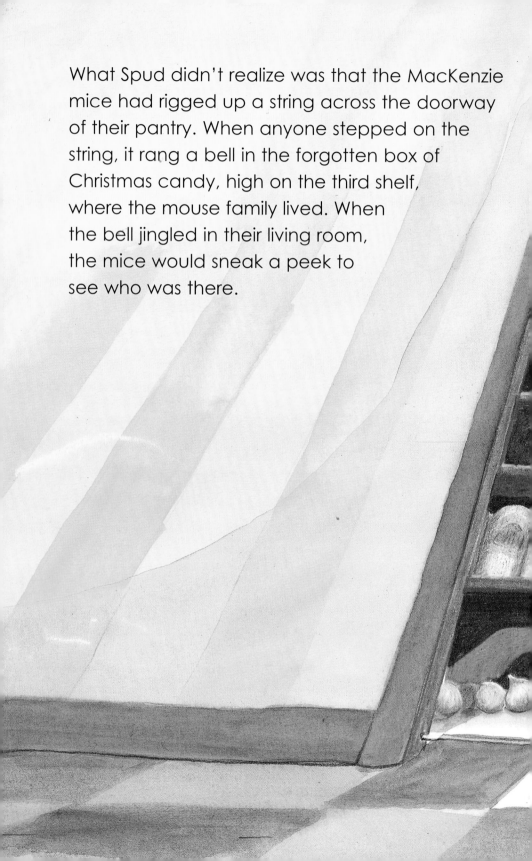

What Spud didn't realize was that the MacKenzie mice had rigged up a string across the doorway of their pantry. When anyone stepped on the string, it rang a bell in the forgotten box of Christmas candy, high on the third shelf, where the mouse family lived. When the bell jingled in their living room, the mice would sneak a peek to see who was there.

"Oh my!" squealed Meatball to her brothers when she looked down and saw Spud. "It's a rat!"

Soccer and Stinky scampered to the window to see for themselves. Their parents had gone to the market and wouldn't be back until lunchtime.

"Take care of each other," Dad had reminded them as he and Mrs. MacKenzie headed out the door with the twins.

"Look, Stinky," whispered Soccer, "he's sniffing the air."

"What should we do?" Stinky asked his brother.

"Meatball, burrow into your room and stay there!" Soccer ordered. "Stinky, get our rubber bands and the bag of lima beans. And hurry!"

Within minutes, Stinky came back toting the rubber bands. "Where are the beans?" Soccer asked, keeping one eye on Spud.

"Well, I . . . uh . . . sorta ate them last night," Stinky confessed.

"Stinky!"

"Sorry."

"Well, we'd better think fast because Spud's headed in our direction!"

Spud was now on the first shelf. He was stacking up tuna fish cans to make stairs up to the second shelf.

"**PSST**, Soccer . . . **PSST**, Soccer," came a whisper from behind him.

"Meatball! I told you to burrow into your room!" Soccer said when he saw his sister's polka-dotted tail peeking out from behind the door.

"I know, Soccer, but I have something you need," Meatball promised.

"Not now, Sister, we're in danger!"

"But I have trinkets for your rubber bands!"

"What? Where?" Soccer turned around.

Meatball handed her shoebox of goodies to him.

"But, Meatball, this is your favorite collection. . . ."

"I know, but I think they'll work to keep us safe. Besides, what else do we have?"

Soccer knew that Meatball was right. He'd have to use them. The trinkets were treasures that Meatball had been collecting for a long time. There were buttons, a pink eraser, a cheese puff, gumdrops, miniature marshmallows, and her latest discovery, a ripe, juicy grape.

Loading up their trinkets and rubber bands, Soccer and Stinky marched up to the roof of their home to protect themselves. Suddenly there was a great roar as Spud jumped onto the third shelf. The loud noise so frightened the brothers that they dropped everything.

Spud laughed aloud, knowing he had the mice trapped. Soccer and Stinky backed up to the edge of the roof, their knees knocking. Then just as Spud leaned down to show the boys his pointy teeth, Meatball snuck up unnoticed and plopped on the grape, sending a spray of grape juice flying in Spud's direction.

Bull's-eye! She hit Spud right between his bushy eyebrows, causing him to stop and rub his wet face. The boys grabbed their rubber bands, reloaded, and let them fly.

ZAP! Soccer smacked the bully rat on the ear with a cheese puff.

ZING! Stinky hit Spud with a purple gumdrop.

"GRRRRR!" was Spud's reply.

Then Soccer thumped the bully with a spinning marshmallow, and Stinky got him with a yellow button. But before they could reload, Spud rushed toward the brothers and grabbed them. "You little pipsqueaks! I gotcha now!"

No sooner had Spud spoken than a pink, flying object bounced off the tip of his gnarly nose. Spud let out a mighty yelp and dropped the mice. He sat down with a thud. "My nose! My nose!" he howled. "Why'd you do that? I wasn't really gonna hurt nobody."

"Well, you sure did act like it!" Meatball announced. Soccer and Stinky turned to see who had rescued them. Meatball had pulled back a spoon, loaded it with the eraser, and flung it into the air.

"I was just—**SNIFF**—just trying to scare you guys—**SNIFF**." replied Spud.

"Well, you don't seem so scary now," Stinky teased.

"And you guys don't seem so little now," Spud admitted, getting up to walk away.

Spud's nose had swollen up to look like a Christmas tree light bulb. He stood up and headed down the shelves and back to the garage.

"Spud, just because we're smaller than you doesn't give you the right to be mean to us," Meatball began, throwing down a tissue to him. "Bullies aren't welcome here. When you learn to be kind, maybe you can come back and play with us."

As soon as their parents returned, Soccer, Stinky, and Meatball began talking all at once. "One at a time, please," instructed their dad.

So, taking turns, each mouse told what had taken place.

"Thank you for working together to send Spud on his way," Dad began, after hearing what had happened. "Standing up to a bully can be tough, but sometimes it's the only thing that helps."

"But, Daddy, I still felt sorry for Spud—even though I knew he was trying to scare us," Meatball said.

"I love your compassion, Meatball, but it's still good to be careful, especially when you don't trust someone," Dad explained.

"You know what else I learned, Dad?" Soccer added. "I learned girls can be as brave as boys." Soccer turned to his sister. "Thanks, Meatball. Stinky and I really needed your help."

"I'm so proud of all of you," Dad said with a smile. "Bullies can be big and scary, but remember, children: big is not about how tall you get, but how much you grow up on the inside."

Meatball was so happy, she ran to her room, put on her tutu, and spun around in circles. And inside, she felt herself growing up.